Forever M

by

Ann Cunningham

PublishNation
www.publishnation.co.uk

Contents

Chapter 1

"Meeting My Spirit Guide"

I had met a lovely lady, and through several sessions with her I had embarked on a journey of spiritual development. Today we would be working on my past life and meeting my spirit guide.

I got myself settled on the sofa and was ready. Like the sessions before, I relaxed by taking deep breaths. I breathed in and out very slowly and then, on the third breath, I began to feel my head slowly moving forward. I was not asleep but was drifting away. At one point, I felt a very strong energy in front of me. I became very hot. I was told that the person in front of me was my guide and he had come forward to meet me. I asked politely if he could move back slightly, and within a second I felt okay again.

I continued to breathe deeply and then I heard a song playing. "Every Breath You Take"; I recognised it straight away. I wasn't sure why it was playing but I stayed calm, and then I started to receive images. The image I was first given was of a soldier, a very tall man with a moustache and in full uniform. Standing next to him was a nurse. She was much smaller than he was and a lot younger. She was holding a small silver tray. On the tray was a little white cloth.

As the images came into my mind, I told my tutor, and she explained to me that the man was my spirit guide and the lady who was the nurse was me. I was being shown in pictures who I was in a past life.

The whole experience lasted for over an hour and I was given many more images and saw other people as well.

The following chapters have been written so that you, the reader, will get to know all of the people I encountered on that day, and why I heard that song.

Chapter 2

"The Yellow Dress"

The only time that I ever felt loved was when I went to church. My teacher, Mrs Forbes, would stand outside and welcome everyone in. She always spoke to me and asked me how I was. She had light brown hair and wore a black bonnet that had ribbons that hung down either side.

My parents would bring me to church and then, after the service, I was allowed to go and play. We had, in front of the house, a small courtyard, and in the middle was a huge cross. If you looked out of the bedroom window you could see it. It was the only time I felt happy. Before going to church, we all had to put on our best clothes. I had a dress, a yellow one. It was beautiful and had a small white collar. A friend of my mother's had given it to her for me. When I wore it I would play for hours in it, turning around and around. I didn't have any other siblings or very many friends, so I played alone.

As it got darker, my mother would shout to me to come in. I did as she said, and I was told to go upstairs and to put my dress away. I did as she said and before I closed the door, I hugged my dress one more time.

I was only allowed downstairs for a short time. Father was sat in his chair close to the fire and was mending old shoes, and mother was sat opposite him. She had some sewing and was busy making a gift for a new baby that had been born. Nobody spoke and it was silent. The only thing you could hear was the fire crackling. As I looked at both of them, I hoped that they would talk to me or even ask me to pull up a small stool and join them, but they never did. They did love me, I knew that, but just sometimes I felt invisible to them. If I did speak, I was told to be quiet and then they just carried on with their work.

Mother was far stricter than Father. He and I were closer than Mother and I. When he did have the time, he would tell me little stories. I sat on his knee and he would sing to me. At Christmas time he made me some little toys from wood and hid them so I wouldn't find them. My mother was very different; she did take care of me, but was always running around doing things for other people and helping when a new baby had been born. Now and again I had a few girls and boys to play with. Mother would have them to stay as their own mother was resting. So many of the families had as many as eight children, and yet my family only had one.

As I got older, my father became poorly, and I helped to look after him. My mother had very little time for him. She would just stand at the door while I sat on his bed talking to him and making him laugh. She never smiled very much, and it was sad, because she did have a big heart and could be very funny.

Then one day I was looking after my father and she came in and started shouting at me. She said that I needed to find work. We had very little money now that Father could not work as much as he used to. I couldn't stop crying and sobbed and sobbed. My father tried to console me, but my mother told him that we had no choice and that I must do as she said. I started to think about what I could do and then I remembered that Mrs Forbes had always said that I would make a good nurse. This is something that my father also used to say to me.

I left the house and went to see Mrs Forbes. She was sorry about what had happened between my mother and I. "She said that my mother did love me, but she was afraid and worried for the family." We spoke about nursing and then I made my way to our local hospital. They were recruiting for new nurses and also needed nurses to go overseas to France. I had never left home before and had always been in this town. After talking to the nurses, I decided that the best thing would be for me to leave. I was told when I would be departing and given all the details. When I got home, I told my mother and father. My mother hugged and kissed me and my father cried. He didn't want to see his little girl go but knew we had very little choice.

Before I was due to leave, I would make sure to visit our friends and go to the parks and canals, as I loved to walk and explore the town.

Chapter 3

"Lawrence The Painter"

Lawrence was never going to be the kind of man to settle for just one woman. He spent most of his days in the bars, drinking until all hours until he was the last one.

He hadn't always been like this. Lawrence had married quite young. His wife had had a very troublesome birth and after a few days, she sadly passed away. It was a difficult time for Lawrence and he had to learn to care for his son. There was never anyone else for Lawrence; he had loved his wife deeply and now that she had gone, he was all alone.

He was a painter and painted most days; this is how I came to meet him. I was taking a walk early one morning and he was painting along the riverside. He had his easel set up. It was warm but pleasant, and not a cloud in the sky. As I walked past he said hello to me. I was quite shy and spoke very quietly when I replied. He had a lovely smile and curly black hair.

"Where are you from?" I asked.

"I am from France. My family is still living there, and I am here, as I am studying painting. I will be leaving next week to head back."

"I will also be going to France next week, as I am needed in the hospitals. I am a nurse. Maybe if I see you at the port we can talk again."

"I would very much like that."

"I am Edith."

"I am Lawrence. Nice to have met you, my dear."

A week later, I stood at the port waiting for my ship, but I could see no sign of Lawrence. The ship arrived and after all the passengers had got off, I made my way onto it. I found a spot to sit and settled down. Just as I did this, a voice said, "You'd better come inside, miss. It's very cold and

I did as he said
blanket for the journ
was worth it, as I

A loud sound
arrived. I thank
off the boat an

"Hello. Y
To whic
"I am
asked to
We
stepp
we h

pla
jour
of th
would
into m
Afte
few str
me in.
"You
upstairs
you have

omorrow would be an
orning. There wasn't
hings wrapped in a
noon tea and then
t, and headed out
ngs and needed
w days, there

apel. There
el looked
t inside
s very
o had

nd
ple
se I
had
e it. I
I had
the air
d over,
he last
tuffy. I
gs with
up.

Chapter 4

"A Time for Love and War"

I'm here. My first day at the hospital. I've never really tended to anyone before. I helped Aunt Dotty once in her home when she was caring for Uncle Harry, but that's about it. Also more recently, looking after my father. Nursing training consisted of baths, bedpans, and the occasional bandage. I had no idea what was going to happen, but I was ready.

"Morning, Edith. We are so happy to see you today. So sorry to hear about the old gentleman. He was a dear old man and looked after lots of our nurses over the years."

"Yes, he was very sweet. I only met him yesterday, but could tell he was a gentleman. What will I be doing today?"

"I thought you could start on the top floor. We have some men who stay there all the time. A nice way for you to get familiar with the place."

I made my way upstairs, hung up my coat, and then entered the ward. The sister in charge was called Emily.

"You must be Edith. I am Emily, the ward sister."

"Very pleased to meet you, Emily."

"Have you been in France long?"

"No, I only arrived yesterday. Just finding my feet."

"Best find them quick; you will be on them long enough."

I laughed inside to myself. Emily was a bit of a joker and I liked to have a laugh. I felt at ease and thought that she and I would get on just fine. Emily showed me around. She introduced me to each patient and while she was doing that, I was taking notes as we went from bed to bed. It must be hard for all these men to be here, never knowing when they will return home, or not in some cases.

As I reached the final bed, I was introduced to Alfred. Alfred had been here for quite some time.

"Excuse me, miss, but could I ask a favour of you?"

"Okay," I replied.

"I can't read or write and saw you writing in your book. Would you write a letter to my wife for me, if I tell you what to write in it?"

"Yes, of course."

Alfred had told me that his wife did visit but not very often, as the transport here was not every week and she lived a few towns away.

"Are you married, miss?"

"No, not me. I haven't found that special someone who will sweep me off my feet. Have you been married a long time, Alfred?"

"Yes, I met my wife when I was seventeen, we courted for two years, and then got married. It was nothing fancy. A few friends, family, a cake, and a good old sing-song."

"Where did you meet?"

"My wife had been overseas to visit relatives and we met on her return. We had a festival in the town and she was handing out flowers, and I was cooking fresh fish and making bread. She needed my help and we got talking. She was lovely: fair hair, blue eyes, and she was tall and slim. She made me feel at home and we got on like a house on fire. We saw each other most days and then I asked her out and she said yes."

"How did you know you loved her and wanted to marry her?"

"Every day I thought of her and wanted to be with her. I had never met anyone who touched my heart the way that she did. If there is such a thing as being made for each other, then Ingrid and I are a perfect match."

"Maybe one day I will meet someone like that."

As I finished talking to Alfred, someone was tugging at my sleeve.

"Please, miss, can you help me?"

"Yes—it's Jerome, isn't it?"

"Yes, miss."

I helped him as best I could; he couldn't see very well and needed lots of guidance. I took him back to his bed and helped him get settled.

"Come quick," a voice shouted down the corridor. "Someone has been shot and you are needed on the ground floor side ward."

I ran quickly down three flights of stairs and into the side ward through the double doors. There was blood everywhere and Matron was covered.

"Get that linen and tear it into strips and then pass it to me," were the instructions from Matron. I did as I was told and handed them to her.

"Now watch what I do."

She started to wrap the linen very tightly around the arm, and then again and again.

"Where is the bullet? Someone said he had been shot."

"Went straight through. Lucky for him, it missed his main arteries. He will have a nasty mark and scar, but he will live."

The man was then taken to the main ward.

I got to work and helped Matron clean and scrub the place. There was blood on the floor, up the walls, and on the bed. It took a while, but we eventually got it looking as good as new again.

"So, how has your first day been, Edith?"

"It's been okay. I'm finding my way around and getting to know everyone."

"I saw just now that you weren't fazed by what you saw. That's what we need. It was bad today, but it will get worse over the coming days and weeks. Are you up for it, Edith?"

"I am."

"Then meet me here tomorrow at eight. We are going to the Chapel of Rest for a service. One of our sergeants has died and we will say farewell. It will also give us both a chance to meet the new sergeant."

With that, I quickly went back to helping on the top floor again.

Chapter 5

"Attention"

The Little Chapel of Flowers was packed full and at the back, people were standing for the service. We had come today to pay our respects and bid a final farewell to a man who had served in the Army for many years. He was very well liked and would be missed by many.

We all sang hymns, some in French and some in English. Even if you couldn't speak the language, you could feel the energy in the room and could see how loved this man was.

As the priest said his final words and we gave thanks to God, the soldiers in attendance sang a song to their leader. A song about facing life in all its hurts and turmoils, but knowing that by doing this, we help to safeguard our families and our country. As I looked around, many people were crying and then shaking hands and embracing each other. A fitting end to a wonderful service.

He was then carried out of the church and, as we followed, he was taken to a small graveyard. The priest came and we all held hands. He was then lowered into the ground. As we stood in silence, a little old man started to play the accordion and then, in turn, we threw flowers into the grave.

As I looked up, I saw a very tall man talking to the sister in charge of the hospital. He looked very fine in his uniform. The sister had told me that there would be a new Sergeant Major, and I did wonder whether this was him. I didn't have to wonder for very long, as the soldier in question came over to me.

"Hello. I am the acting Sergeant Major Joseph Grinds. And you are…?"

"I am Edith. I have just joined the Augustus Hospital for the Sick, and the lady you were chatting with is my matron."

"That is good to know, as you will be seeing lots of me in the coming weeks. I have been stationed here for the foreseeable future."

"I too will be here long-term. I don't imagine that I will be going back to England for a long time. I do miss home. I live in a little town called Loughborough. Everyone is very friendly and helpful. We have real community spirit."

"How amazing; I too am from that town. My family has lived there most of their lives. I lived in Paget Street before joining the Army."

"I lived on the other side of town. I lived in Gladstone Street, not too far away."

"We will have to catch up again, Edith. We have lots to discuss. Please join us with your matron, as we are heading to a small hall nearby for light refreshments and music."

"That would be lovely, thank you."

As Joseph walked away, I was happy in my heart to have met someone from back home. We didn't know each other at all and had never met before, but somehow, I knew that we would get to know each other, and I was looking forward to it.

Chapter 6

"Cabaret de Dance"

Today, Saturday, I decided to venture out. The street I was living on had a bar across the road. In the day it was all shut up and you would think that it was closed. At night it came alive—bright lights, music, and lots of women walking up and down the road, asking people to come in and join in the merriment.

I had awoken quite early and, on doing so, had a strange feeling in my stomach. It was one of those feelings whereby something was going to happen or something had already happened. It was almost as though I felt loved by someone, but that was silly as I was single and hadn't met anyone for years. The last man I stepped out with was more interested in his farm and animals than he was in having a female companion.

After having breakfast in a small café, I walked along a little street. It was all uphill and very steep. I was out of breath and found myself stopping for a moment. Just as I did, a familiar figure came walking towards me. Was I dreaming or did that man look very like someone I had met back home? As he got closer, my heart was pounding and I felt quite weak at the knees. A huge smile came over his face and I knew at that moment that it was Lawrence. I had thought about him and had hoped and dreamed that we would meet again, but it was just a dream and in reality, I never imagined it would ever happen.

"Hello, Lawrence; so lovely to see you again. I did look for you at the port but you were not there."

"No, my dear, I was delayed by a few days, but I am here now. I would like to introduce you to my son. Edith, this is Christophe. He is three years old."

I bent down so that myself and Christophe were at the same eye level.

"Hello, Christophe. I am Edith and I am a nurse from England."

"Say hello to the nice lady?"

Christophe looked at me and smiled. He was a little shy. He looked very like Lawrence.

"Off you go, Christophe, and play."

And off he went, skipping and running up the street, as myself and Lawrence became reacquainted.

"I am so sorry, Lawrence, about your wife. It must be very hard for both of you."

"It is, but we look after each other and my painting keeps my mind occupied."

"How is your painting coming along?"

"Just fine, Edith. I sold four paintings yesterday and three the day before. A shopkeeper is looking after them for me and he helps to sell them when people visit his shop."

"What is your subject?"

"Women. I like to draw and to paint women. They pose for me in the nude."

I went shy and could feel the blood rush to my cheeks.

"Oh, Edith, you are such a sweet rose, aren't you? A precious thing that has been carefully looked after and nurtured."

"I don't really know, but I do know that I haven't met a painter before, nor have I met someone that paints nudes."

"What do you like to do, Edith?"

"I like to sing, but I am too shy and nervous to do it in public. I would love to be on a little stage and sing, not to lots of people, just a few. And dance maybe, that would be nice."

"Maybe someday it will happen for you."

"I hope so."

"I must go, Edith. I have lots to do today. I am starting some new paintings and need to buy some materials. Christophe is going to stay with some dear friends down the road over the weekend while I work. Goodbye, my dear."

"Goodbye, Lawrence."

I went to the park and sat and watched the people come and go. Ladies and gentlemen holding hands and children playing. There was a bandstand and people gathered around it to listen to the music. It was a place that was filled with flowers and trees, and you could hear the birds singing. A little piece of heaven. I was so glad that I found this place. The long hours at the hospital, along with the awful things that had happened to the men there, had taken their toll on me. The park helped me forget for a short while and I was able to relax.

After my walk out, I returned to my lodgings and took a short nap. I wasn't sleeping that well at the moment and lay on top of the bed. By the time I had awoken it was night-time and I could hear music coming from across the way. I decided that I would go and find out what this place was. As I stood outside, I peered through the window, hoping not to be caught. Women danced onstage and sang songs that I had never heard before. I thought I hadn't been seen, "but one of the ladies did see me"and brought me in via a side door.

"You look too prim and proper to be here. Come with me, you can watch from the back."

I thanked her and she offered me a stiff drink.

"Here, get this down you. You're gonna need it."

"Why will I need this?"

"Let's just say it's better you relax and enjoy your night."

I did as she said. I knocked it back. I wobbled for a moment and then got my balance again.

"Wow," I said. "That's gone to my toes, and back to my head."

The costumes that they wore were amazing. Tight corsets, stockings, and shoes that had diamonds on them.

I had enjoyed watching them. As I turned to go out the door, I saw someone sat all on his own. The table was full of empty glasses and women surrounded him. They would sit on his knee for a few moments, kiss him, and then get up and walk away. This happened a few times while I was watching.

That drink had made me feel brave, so I walked over to the table and sat down. He lifted his head, expecting to see another dancer or waitress, I suppose, and instead saw me.

"Oh my days; what are you doing here?"

"Well, not working, if that's what you thought?"

"Oh no, I could never imagine you working in a place like this."

"I had heard the music for many nights but never had the courage to come in. Until tonight, that is. Why are you here?"

"I come here in the day sober and meet the girls. If I like any of them, then I paint them. At night I come to drown my sorrows and forget the past, my wife, my child…just forget."

"The women, are any of them with you?"

"Some are friends and some are lovers, but I don't love any of them. I only love my wife. Please don't think badly of me."

"I wouldn't, and I won't. I am leaving now. Shall I walk you home, Lawrence?"

"I will be okay. I will stay a little longer; the night is still young, and I have just got started."

I hated leaving him there and wanted to stay, but I had an early start again tomorrow. The more and more I saw Lawrence, the more my heart was beginning to fill with joy and feelings for this man. I had only seen him a few times, but I remembered what Alfred had said about Ingrid. Could I be having the same feelings that they did when they were starting to fall in love?

Only time would tell. I now knew where to find him, and he was never ever very far away.

Chapter 7

"Can I Call You?"

I had been working hard for many months in the hospital and had very little time to myself. I missed the simple life and just being able to go out and have fun. There was no time for fun here, and the many hours I spent in the hospital left me drained and, some days, unable to think straight.

I had seen Joseph on and off in the hospital and he came on many occasions to inspect the wards. Some of his men were in here and he paid them all a visit to see how they were progressing. Each of the soldiers, in turn, would try their best to get up out of the bed as he came by. They wanted to stand up and show him respect because, after all, he was their leader. Joseph, however, had a softer and gentler side to him that I had seen from afar. He would tell the men to stand down and to return to normal duties. This was his way of telling them to relax and take it easy. You soon pick up the language of the Army and what it all means in our world.

Late one evening, as I was in the side office, I saw Joseph limping past. He grabbed hold of the stairs and almost fell over. I ran out to tend to him.

"Joseph, are you okay?"

"Yes and no. My leg keeps playing up."

"Let me take a look for you."

"No, that won't be necessary. It's nothing."

"I insist and won't take no for an answer. Come with me now."

"For a small woman, you can be forceful when you want to, can't you?"

"If it helps to get your leg seen, then yes."

We walked a few yards and I asked him to sit on the bed and pull himself around. After he had done this, I gently rolled up his trouser leg and removed his sock. The trousers were easy, but the sock was stuck and I had to cut it off. The smell was awful, and his foot had started to look black.

"How long has your foot been like this, Joseph?"

"Quite a few months. It wasn't too bad at first, but the pain has become unbearable. The sister in the hospital has been treating it. I come late at night when everyone on the wards is asleep. I don't want anyone to find out."

"Do not worry, I will take care of you and it will go no further, I promise."

"You are very kind, Edith, to me and my soldiers. I see you going back and forth, helping them and writing letters for them to their loved ones."

"I am a long way from home, so keeping busy and giving comfort to others helps me and helps them at the same time."

"There you go. I have bathed your leg and foot and strapped it up for you."

"Thank you, Edith. Edith?"

"Yes."

"Can I call you?

As I looked deeply into his eyes and face, there was only one answer that I could give to this strong brave man.

"Yes, oh yes, Joseph."

As I said those words, he leant down and kissed me gently. I hugged him and in that moment, we came to be the closest of friends. As I let go, he walked away, and just before he left, he took one more glance back at me. I smiled, and in my heart, I was overjoyed. I was happy and had found a great man in Joseph.

It was a few weeks, but the call did come, and every week we walked arm in arm around the grounds of the hospital. It was set in a very picturesque place with woods and trees. There was an old library that we visited; it was quiet, and we were able to talk in private. Joseph loved to read and spent most of his spare time in here. I myself didn't read an awful lot, but I did like to write, and I think this is one of the reasons that I would pen letters for the soldiers.

Later, in the evenings, we would sit in his private house and I would make dinner for him and do a few things around the house. He was struggling, I could see that, and so I offered. A few months later, he asked If I would be his personal assistant and nurse. My duties would be to take care of him and I would also live in his house. I thought about it for a few days and then accepted. He was on his own and I knew that he had no one else.

We were both from the same town and where we came from, we took care of each other. Your neighbour wasn't just the person next door, but many streets away also.

I moved all of my belongings from where I was staying and moved into the little house with Joseph. The sister in charge was very happy and she had already found a replacement for me. I wouldn't be too far away and in times of emergency, I had agreed to help out.

This was a new start for me and for Joseph. Where our working relationship and friendship went, only time would tell.

Chapter 8

"A Portrait of Beauty"

A grand event had been arranged as Joseph was now officially a Sergeant Major, and to celebrate this and lift morale, a dinner and dance had been arranged.

Each of us would take a partner to the ball. I hadn't expected to be asked, as I wasn't part of the Army, a wife, or even a loved one. Joseph had asked me to go with him as I was his personal aid and he needed me by his side. I was very honoured to be asked, but I didn't know what to wear and the clothes that I had were not fit for a ball. I did, of course, know of someone who could help me.

I set off and went to the Cabaret de Dance. I had met Gabby a while ago and loved the style of some of the clothes she and the others wore. Maybe she could help me?

I entered the building and two men were arguing and shouting. I couldn't make out what they were talking about, but their faces were red and sweaty and at one point, one of them slammed his fist on the table. I felt uneasy, and then Gabby appeared.

"Hello, Edith, have you come to join us on stage?"

"Oh, no, I haven't. I have been invited to a grand ball, but have nothing to wear and thought you may be able to help me find something."

"I don't think that any of the dresses that we wear would be appropriate, but Adele, our seamstress, may be able to help you. I will take you to her; she is just around the corner."

We both left and quickly arrived at where Adele was living—a small building, with very small windows and a chimney that had smoke coming out of it.

"She gets cold and has been unwell for a while. Her chest hurts and the warm air helps her."

"Has she seen anyone about it?"

"Yes, she has, but there is nothing anyone can do for her. She is bedridden some days and has no energy, as she cannot breathe very well."

Gabby knocked on the door and a lady opened it.

"Morning, Adele. I have brought you someone who needs your help. Her name is Edith and she is a nurse."

"Welcome, Edith. Do come in."

As I entered the house we went straight through and into the back. The room was full of dresses, corsets, and petticoats.

"So, how can I help you, Edith?"

"I have been invited to a ball. It is for the newly appointed sergeant major, Joseph Grind. I am his personal assistant. I don't have anything to wear that would suit the occasion."

"Let me have a look here for you. I am sure I can find something that would fit you."

She searched through many different dresses and then finally came across a beautiful black dress. It had a silk collar and long chiffon sleeves. The skirt of it was long, black netting over the top and black satin underneath. On the dress itself were tiny roses that had been handstitched on.

"Try this on, Edith?"

I tried it on and it was lovely. A little too long for me, but Adele had her pins to hand and started to take the hem up.

"When is the ball, Edith?"

"Next Thursday evening."

"Come tomorrow and I will have It ready. We can do a final fit for you. I also have a little bag and also stockings for you."

"I have forgotten shoes. I need shoes also. I am so sorry; do you have any?"

"I have a few pairs. Let's see what suits you. Here we go."

They were perfect. A small heel that I could walk in and also dance in if I was lucky enough to be asked. The top had a big bow on it.

"How much do I owe you, Adele, for everything?"

"As you are a friend of Gabby's, there is no charge. Besides, it isn't every day I get to make a dress for a lady, Edith."

"That is so very kind. Have you been making and doing alterations for long?"

"My mother taught me and then when I came here I met Gabby and we worked together. I was a dancer and singer on stage for many years, but I became ill and had to retire. I now make all the dresses for the girls in the shows."

As I looked around, a picture hanging above the fireplace caught my eye.

"Is that you, Gabby?"

"Yes, it is. I was twenty-five when it was painted, about five years ago. A painter comes in most nights and he asked if he could paint my portrait. Lawrence is his name. A lovely young man, but very troubled, and he has a son."

"I have met Lawrence. I met him back home in England, but I haven't seen him in a while. Your portrait is so lovely; I would love to have one of me."

"Why don't you ask him? He is living above a shop in town; I have his address here somewhere. All these dresses, you can never find anything. Found it. Here you go. Take this, and if you struggle to find it, ask in the square. People are very helpful around here."

"Thank you. I will."

I said goodbye and told her that I would be back tomorrow, But first, there was someone I really needed to see: Lawrence. It had been a while, but my stomach fluttered every time I thought of him. I didn't know why, but I was going to find out.

Chapter 9

"Wishing You Were Mine"

In the middle of the square was a little old shop. It sold everything from tablecloths to tables themselves. Inside, the rooms were set out just like a house, with comfy chairs and ornaments. All of it was for sale.

The man in the shop asked if he could help and I replied that I was there to see the painter, Lawrence. He showed me a staircase and I was told to follow it up and knock on the door.

I hadn't really thought about what I was going to say when I saw him, and each step I took, I could feel my heart pounding and getting faster and faster. My nerves started to go a bit and I gasped a few times for breath. I did think about turning back and leaving, but I pushed myself to keep going. I said to myself, "I am here now. This is it."

As I took the last step, I knocked on the door. There was no answer, so I tried again, a bit harder.

"Okay, okay, I am coming," I could hear from inside.

As the door started to open I stood there as still as could be until we were face to face, and as I sighed, I breathed out the words, "Hello, Lawrence, how are you?"

"Edith, what a surprise. I never expected to see you standing there. Come in."

As I entered the room I realised, it was a painting studio, bedroom, and living room all in one. There was paint and pictures everywhere. Some had been finished, and others only half.

"Please come and sit down. Just move all that stuff onto the table and I will see if I have some tea for us."

"You don't have to, Lawrence."

"It's fine, my dear, I will only be a minute."

He was true to his word. He brought everything in and then

heated the water over a small fire in the fireplace.

"So, what brings you here, Edith?"

"I was with Gabby at Adele's house and she had this portrait on the wall. When I asked who painted it, she told me it was you. I have always wanted to have my portrait painted."

We sat and chatted for a while. I heard some of it but not all of it. My eyes were fixed on his all the time he spoke. We chatted for what seemed like hours and we never ran out of things to say. We laughed quite a bit and he held my hand for most of the time. Joseph often held my hand, but this felt different to me. Different because I felt like when we chatted, our hearts became whole. That Lawrence somehow was a part of me, and me of him.

I had heard about knowing when you meet the right one and falling in love, etc., but had never experienced it until now. All the time I was with him, I never wanted to think about it ending and that at some point I would have to leave and go back home.

Joseph was a kind man and I did love him and cared for him, but I was starting to understand the difference between loving someone and being in love, and I knew that I was in love with Lawrence. How he felt about me, I did not know, and I didn't want to say anything as it might spoil things.

I stayed for a further few hours and then it was time to leave.

"I must go now, Lawrence. I have to attend to some patients before going home. I have really enjoyed seeing you again. I have had the best time this afternoon talking."

"I have also enjoyed our time together. It was a total surprise to see you, but a very nice one indeed. I have agreed to paint a new portrait for the Sergeant Major that you care for, Joseph, as a gift for him at the ball next week. It is almost finished; would you like to see it?"

"Oh, yes."

As he pulled up the cloth that was covering the painting, there he was, the man who I take care of and look after. He looked so grand and smart and Lawrence had captured all of his features, even a small scar he had at the corner of one of his eyes. It seemed quite odd, standing with Lawrence, looking at Joseph.

"Will you be at the ball next week, Edith?"

"Me? Oh no, I am just an assistant."

I had lied, of course. I didn't want him to know I was going; I wanted to surprise him yet again, and when he saw me with my hair done and my new dress, I wanted him to see the woman that had been hiding away in these old clothes and nurse's uniform for what seemed like decades.

"Shame that you will not be there."

Lawrence then covered up the painting, and before I left, he handed me something. A rose. A fresh-smelling pink rose. He had picked it fresh that day. It was in a vase as I came in.

"For you, Edith. A beautiful thing, just like you."

As I looked down and held the rose close to me, he gently lifted my chin and kissed me. The kiss seemed to last forever and my stomach had butterflies in it.

"Goodbye, my dear Edith."

"Goodbye, Lawrence."

I hurried down the steps with a spring in my step and a smile on my face. I was in love; I loved him, and I now knew he loved me too.

I couldn't wait now for the ball, and to see him once again.

Chapter 10

"Dance With Me"

All night, I tossed and turned, thinking about the ball tomorrow. I really needed to get some sleep; it was going to be a busy day. I had to work and also go and get my dress for the evening. I kept picturing in my mind what I would look like in it.

I finally got to sleep for about two hours, and then I was up and changed and headed downstairs. It was still dark outside and I always felt frightened about the dark. I don't know what it was that made me scared, but as a young girl, I would scream in my sleep and my mother would come in and try and soothe me. Sometimes I would end up in her be____ ___til I fell asleep, and then she would gently carry me b__ _____asn't asleep for very long and as soon as she left ___ _____ake up once more. This went on for years until on___ _____ed that I should have a night light, and until this d___

Joseph was sat at ___ _____had tea and breakfast. He would be doing his ro___ _____we all had to meet in the courtyard. He wanted _____ning's event and to wish everyone well.

I cleaned away all ___ ___d then went upstairs. I had promised Joseph t___ ____ his finest suit, shoes, and hat were all ready _____rted at 8 p.m. but we needed to be there at ___ ___nd arrangements. His shoes needed a good p_____d at this, but I knew that Ted, one of the s___ ___ As he took his early morning walk around t___ ___ get his attention.

"Ted, I have a favou___

"What would that b___

"I am not very go___ ___nd wondered if you would help me? They a___

"As it is you, Edith, I will come now. It won't take long and I will show you so that you can do them the next time."

So we went back to the house and I fetched the shoes from upstairs. Ted quickly got to work and polished them so that you could see every hair on your head in them. I had watched everything he had done and, so that I didn't forget, I made notes as well, and a little drawing. I'm not much of an artist, but my little picture would do and it would help me later on.

I had now got to go and get my dress. This was the most exciting part of the day for me; even the ball didn't excite me as much as going to see my little dress. I hope it's ready and it fits.

I ran down the street and finally made my way to Adele's house. I knocked on the door and there she was, smiling at me.

"Come in, come in, Edith. I have everything ready for you."

She had indeed. The bag she gave to me was just perfect. It matched my dress and had the same little roses on it. The shoes I had tried on last time, and so I knew they would be okay, but what about the dress?

"Here you go, Edith. Go and

I went behind a small scr   om and threw the
clothes I took off over it. I   n over my head, so
as not to split it, and then   my body. It fitted. I
sighed, a sense of relief, a   behind the screen.

"Let me see you in thi

I walked towards the   hoes just before I got
there. I caught a glimps   mach went all funny.
Was that really me?

"Oh, Edith, you lo   seen you a few times
now and could never   look so perfect. How
do you feel? And do y

As I looked at my   le tear fell down over
my cheek. I had so w   like a lady for so long,
and now, with the he   ke a different person.
Each rose on the dre   and the bows on the
shoes had tiny beads   r just an ordinary girl,
but a fine-looking w   ut tonight at the ball,
except for all the righ

As 7 p.m. approached, I made the final touches to my hair and put a tiny bit of rouge on my cheeks and lips. I couldn't afford anything else, so Gabby gave me a few things.

I could hear Joseph downstairs, marching up and down and saying his speech, and then he would say, "Oh no, that's not right," and start again.

I finally came downstairs and there, waiting at the bottom, was Joseph. I have never seen him look so startled before.

"Are you feeling okay, Joseph?"

"Yes, yes I am. I am okay. I mean, good lord! Edith, is that really you?"

"I know. It's a bit of a shock, isn't it?"

"Edith, you look radiant."

What a lovely thing for Joseph to say to me. I had never heard him speak with such passion before; only about his Army life.

"Everyone will be jealous of me tonight, Edith, when they see that I have you on my arm."

I blushed. Even with the rouge on my face, you could still see the glowing cheeks through it. I didn't reply, and we made our way to the hall where the ball was being held. When we got inside, we were greeted by other soldiers and a man came up to you with a tray filled with small glasses. I'm not sure what it was, but all the ladies were drinking it, so I took one and thanked the man.

As the hall filled up, we were then all taken into a second room. There was a top table and Joseph and I were escorted to it. I sat next to him and some of the more senior soldiers of the regiment were also on this table. The tables were arranged in lines around the room so that the space in the middle could be used for dancing.

As we ate, we chatted, and then, at the end, a man stood up and said a few words. He gave thanks to everyone for coming and then spoke about how he had come to know Joseph. Joseph then took his turn and he gave a perfect speech. We raised our glasses to the new Sergeant Major.

Just as we had finished, the doors flew open and in walked Lawrence. He had something under his arm. Another man set up an easel and then Lawrence placed the object on it. I had already seen the picture before, but I wondered what it would look like now it had been finished. As Lawrence unwrapped it, he congratulated Joseph and said that as a gift to him, he had painted his portrait so that everyone in years to come would know who he was. The image was even more like Joseph than the last time I saw it, and everyone commented on how wonderful it was and what a talented man Lawrence was.

The lights were now dimmed and a band played on stage. They had an amazing female singer. Her voice carried all the way to the back of the room and when she sang, the whole place came alive." People were starting to dance. Now and then, someone would ask someone else for a dance."?

Joseph and I danced a few times and I did have a dance with Ted. He had helped me out and it was the least I could do.

As I waltzed around the room, I stopped, and there in front of me was Lawrence.

"Edith, may I have this next dance?"

"Yes, Lawrence, you may."

As he took me in his arms, with each word that the singer sang, we became closer and closer. His eyes were fixed on mine and they never moved an inch. Just as the song came to an end, he whispered to me, "You are like a new fragrance that has just been bottled and released for the first time. An aroma that fills every pore with beauty and elegance. Since I first saw you, I knew that there was something about you. You gripped my heart and I have not felt love like that, not even with my wife. I cannot get you out of my mind. I think of you always."

"I too think of you, Lawrence. Until I met you I never knew what love was. You crept into my life when I was not looking and since then, all I dream of is you."

As we finished talking, I wanted one more dance.

"Lawrence, dance with me?"

"How can I refuse you, Edith?"

We took the centre of the floor and forgot about everyone in the room. It was just the two of us. Two souls that had joined together and become one.

As we finished dancing, there was one more thing on my mind. I had always wanted to be on stage to sing a song. I had sung at home when nobody was around, and a few times with my mother and father.

Lawrence had noticed that I had become a bit quiet and withdrawn.

"Edith, you look sad. Whatever is the matter?"

"All my life I have wanted to sing on a stage and perform, but I have always been too shy."

"Just wait here for a moment."

As I stood there, Lawrence jumped onstage and spoke to the band and the singer. I could see the singer nodding away as he spoke to her. I couldn't hear what they were saying, but she smiled at me and I smiled back.

Lawrence made his way back to me and told me to listen. As the room went quiet, the singer announced the following:

"Ladies and gentlemen, please give a warm welcome to a young lady who is going to sing for us. Please put your hands together for Edith."

Everyone was looking over at me. I felt really hot, and started to shake. The voice in my head kept telling me, *I can't do it. I need to get out of here*. Lawrence could see I was afraid and held my hand.

"Come on, Edith. Walk with me."

I got to the stage and he lifted me up.

I stood there, not knowing what to do. Then the music started to play. I began to sing, a bit croakily at first, and my voice wobbled. Then a big wave of happy thoughts came to me and I sang my little heart out. I put all my soul into it. I forgot about everyone in the room and imagined it was just me.

The song came to the end and I said thank you. There was clapping and cheering and two happy smiling faces looking at me. Lawrence and Joseph, my two friends.

I came off the stage and couldn't believe what I had just done. I thanked Lawrence for making it happen. But the truth was, I had made it happen.

Chapter 11

"All That I Have"

It was a great evening at the ball. Joseph loved his painting, and we decided that the best place for it was in the library. Joseph loved this place and it was such a great place to come and relax.

We had spoken a few times about myself and Lawrence dancing many times, but I just dismissed it and told Joseph that he was just being gentlemanly and not to worry. He did worry about me; he never really let me go many places without him and if I did go into town, he always insisted I had someone with me. I did tell him many times that I did have someone to go with me, but that was for his benefit. I needed to go and walk and feel the air on my face and just be still and quiet. The last thing that I wanted was someone tagging along to spoil all of it for me. I was always grateful to Joseph though. He did care for me, and I knew this.

Joseph's health had taken a turn for the worse. He hadn't been feeling well. His foot and leg were both very swollen. He had seen the matron and she had told him to rest it, but he was having none of it. He still continued to walk the floors of the wards and greet everyone, just the same as always.

As I went for a walk through the grounds I saw him sitting on a bench behind the old wood lodge. I sat beside him, and he had been sweating. The sweat was pouring down his face and his breath was very deep.

"Shall I call for matron and get you to the hospital?"

"No, I will be okay in a moment."

We sat for another half an hour. He kept dozing off and I really got scared. Finally, one of the gardeners came by and I asked for his help to take Joseph home. As we struggled to the door, I managed to get the door open. Both us of us took Joseph into the front room. As the gardener got him settled, I quickly aired the room next door by opening the windows. I changed the bed and then we brought Joseph in and helped him to bed. He settled quite quickly and before long he had fallen asleep. Before the gardener left, I gave him a note to take to Matron to tell her it was urgent.

Within an hour there was a knock on the window. I must have fallen asleep myself, as I woke up in the chair next to Joseph's bed. I could see that it was matron. I let her in and we sat and had tea. I told her what had happened and how he had given me an awful fright. She told me that she had something to tell me about Joseph. I got really upset and couldn't control my fears.

"Edith, he has been poorly for a very long time and he has been getting weaker. We have done our best to help him, but there is nothing more that we can do."

"I don't understand, Matron. I am a little confused."

"He has a weak heart. He may have been born with it, but we cannot tell. When he was a child, he was a very sickly child, and his mother never used to let him go out much. She was afraid that the cold air would get on his chest."

"So how come he came to be in the Army, and such a long way from home, if he was so poorly?"

"As he got older his condition improved greatly. His credentials were excellent, and he had had no symptoms for years. When he joined the Army, he never told them about his heart. He knew that if he did, they would not take him."

"What about his mother? She must have been devastated."

"His mother had passed away about six years or so before he joined the Army, so Joseph decided to sign up. It was very sad that she had died, but she had always prevented him from doing things, and so he made the decision to leave."

"So what happens now?"

"You will have to help him as much as possible. Light meals and plenty of drinks. I will send over help for you as well, so that you can also rest."

I nursed him every day and night. I slept in the chair beside him and had a break when the relief nurse came over.

"Edith, I don't want you to be here every day with me."

"It's fine, Joseph. I agreed to look after you and that is what I will do."

"I know, and I am very grateful, but don't make yourself ill."

As the weeks went by, Joseph went from being active and out every day to being bedridden. We spent the evenings talking, and the soldiers would come to visit him.

Then one night, he took a turn for the worse. The colour drained from his face. He looked at me and told me that he wished that he had more time, but it wasn't to be. As the life within him started to fade, I too felt part of me fade. I held his hand and started to cry. I looked at his face and his eyes had closed. His hand slipped out of mine and he was gone. I kissed his forehead and said, "Goodnight, Joseph. Thank you for taking care of me."

There was a great sadness from everyone. We couldn't believe Joseph had died. He loved his work; he had come to France to help and nurture new soldiers and he did just that.

After the funeral, I couldn't work for a while. I was totally lost without him. We weren't married, nor was he a romantic partner. We had bonded, and I deeply cared for him. All my energy had gone into helping this man, and now I felt alone.

The Army came to the house to clear out his belongings. Among his things was something for me. A letter he had written. He had written it a month or so back, from the date that was on the top of it. There was only one place I was going to read this in, and that was the library. I made my way there and sat at one of the little tables. I carefully unfolded the letter to read what was inside.

Chapter 12

"I'll Always Be with You"

My dearest Edith, I only have a short time left to write this to you. Since you came into my life, everything has changed. I have always been a man of principle. My work and my duties to my country always came first. Then I met you and all of this started to change. You will never really know how much you meant to me. I could never show you or tell you until now. I wish things had been different, but they were not. I became ill and I knew that it would only be a matter of time before I had to say goodbye. You have stood by me, cared for me, and loved me. Nobody has ever done that for me. I never thought I deserved love, as to have love, you must also give it. I never really did, or took the time. Over the past few months, I have watched you grow and grow. I may not be here much longer to care for you, but I promise I will be around, if not in body, but in spirit. A guide to protect you and lead you in the right direction for the rest of your life.

Till we meet again, your friend, Joseph xxx

Chapter 13

"Saving Lawrence"

I was so deeply touched that Joseph had taken the time to write to me. I had never expected it. At night, when I was alone, I would sit on the edge of my bed and hold the letter close to my heart. It was the only thing I had left of him.

Life was hard after he died, and I knew that I could no longer stay in this house on my own, so I spoke to Matron and she found me another place to stay. I had still been active at the hospital, but not as much as before. Everyone had been so kind to me and allowed me a little time to adjust.

It took a long time for me to have a smile back on my face again. I felt guilty and just couldn't enjoy life, not after everything that had happened. Why did he have to die? He was a good man. It was so unfair. Life was so unfair. I struggle with my faith also. I did pray to God, but often found that what I really needed was somehow to make sense of all this. But the answers never came.

One day, as I was in the town, I saw Lawrence. We had not seen each other since the night of the ball. I hadn't thought about him, as I had shut myself off from everything and everyone. He could see that I was upset and he offered to walk with me.

"Edith, can I help in any way?"

"I'm not sure that you can. I have lost a great friend, someone I cared for day and night, and I don't know what to do or how to carry on."

"When my wife died, I thought that my life would never be the same again. I had a small child to care for, and the love of my life had been taken away."

"How did you cope?"

"I didn't at first. I wanted to forget about it. I spent my time drinking my life away. Then the opportunity to go to England came along. I wasn't ready, but something inside me told me to go. If I didn't, I would never move forward in my life. It was a tough decision to leave my child but I was doing this for both of us, and if I worked and studied hard then maybe, just maybe, I could get through."

"I work at the hospital and help everyone else, but I need to find something for me, something that I can be passionate about in the same way you are about your art."

"Is there anything that you can think of?"

"The only thing I like is writing. I write all the letters for the soldiers, but I also have written about the places and the people I meet. I find it all very interesting."

"There you go then. You may not have met the people you write to, but you have touched their lives with your words. You have brought so much joy to many people without even realising it."

"I never thought about it in that way."

"Our lives are not measured in money or what we have, but on how we have changed ourselves and other people around us for the better."

"Thank you, Lawrence. You have really cheered me up. It is so kind of you to help me."

"Edith, you're so lovely. The night of the ball was a special night for me. I love you, Edith. I may not always be around, but your heart will always be in mine."

"Yours will always be in mine."

I leaned forward and put my arms around his neck and kissed him. I smiled and we both laughed. Then a man approached us from the side. I turned around and stood with my back to Lawrence. The man was shouting at Lawrence and waving a weapon about. I was scared but didn't move an inch. As he tried to pull me out of the way, there was a struggle and an almighty bang to my head. I started to fall to the floor, and the man ran away. I could faintly hear Lawrence shouting for help, and telling me to hold on.

"Don't leave me, Edith."

I clung to his coat for dear life as help arrived.

Chapter 14

"In This Life And The Next"

"Hello, Edith. It's a bit cold today, so I've had to put my hat and coat on."

"Christophe sends his love and says he will visit soon."

"My paintings have been accepted into a major gallery and I am overjoyed."

"You always said I would make it. I didn't ever think I would, but your trust and faith in life kept me going."

"I miss you and love you very much."

"You were one special lady, and there will never be another you."

"I have brought your favourite flowers. I've laid them all except one."

"I will take it home and look after it. A reminder of you and my love for you in this life and the next."

"God bless, Edith."

"You will always be...

"Forever my rose."

Chapter 15

"Every Breath You Take"

As I breathed out, I opened my eyes. Tears were falling down my face. I knew that I wasn't dreaming, as I had become very emotional about the whole experience. It was different, because I didn't know these people in person, nor had I made a connection with them, to become so upset.

I was asked about my session and how I felt. I was honest and said that at first, I was a little nervous, but that soon faded. I had enjoyed it and felt that I had got to know my spirit guide, Joseph.

He was someone that I had met in a past life and we had a strong bond and lived a life together. It was my understanding that when he passed over, he had made a commitment to always look after and protect me. To help ensure that I was moving in the right direction. He would always be here for me and I only ever had to ask for his help.

The song "Every Breath You Take" was very significant in all of this. The lyrics of the song, "Every breath you take/Every move you make/I'll be watching you," letting me know he is around.

I have heard that song quite a few times now, often in times of uncertainty in my life and when I have been very low. A message from him to me, to let me know "I am here and all is well, even if it doesn't feel that way."

A guide can't change your life——only you can do that——but they can help you on your path. Similar to an angel, they give you nudges. You know what I mean; you're busy, going about your day, and a thought pops into your head or an idea about something comes out of nowhere. I think it's fair to say we have all said, "Where did that come from?"

The relationships were something that was a total surprise, especially the one with Lawrence. I had only envisaged that I would meet my guide, but to be taken on a journey with three people was quite overwhelming. Finding out that you had loved and were loved by two different men in two different ways was something of a surprise.

I look at the nurse and do I see myself? In some ways, yes: the kind and caring person, but not being a nurse. My theory on this would be that because I had seen so many people in pain and suffering, this is one of the reasons why I am afraid of hospitals and dentists. I can't stand the sight of blood to the point where I feel like I may faint. So nursing would never be an option.

It was interesting that, back then, the nurse never married or had any children, and died quite young. In this life, I have married and had a child. Almost as though the past soul had returned home and, because all of its purpose had not been fulfilled, it was reborn again.

The main reason I had developed my own understanding of spirituality and spiritual gifts was because I had experienced quite a few things myself and wondered what it was about and what it all meant. I won't mention them at this point, as they can be shared another time.

I do hope that everyone that reads this can at least say that they understand more about past lives and spirit guides, even if they don't believe in them.

Much love and thank you for reading this. Ann xx

About the Author

My name is Ann Cunningham and I was born in Loughborough, Leicestershire, at our family home, 15 Oaklands Avenue, on 16 July 1968. I have lived in this town all my life and as I write this, my home is in an old Victorian terrace that was built around 1895.

My parents are both from Ireland. I am an only girl and have three older brothers. I was very quiet and shy when I was younger and I would snuggle up to my parents whenever we were at anyone's house.

My family would often talk about their lives back in Ireland and at Christmas we would all get together at my grandmother's house. It was a night of singing and dancing. We all looked forward to it every year.

I loved to go shopping with my mother. I was always at her side and she would talk away to her friends and introduce me to them. I have never forgotten who they are.

I think for me, all of these experiences have enabled me to become a writer, along with being a good storyteller.

My first experience of writing came about five years ago, when a friend asked if I would like to write on a new art website that he and his family had created. I agreed and found that I had a natural flair when I wrote about great artists and charities that had changed people's lives through art. Through my writing I was able to reach out to many people.

Being creative is something that I really enjoy, and of late I have started to write short stories, poems, and now this first novel of mine.

I would never have been able to do this without the love and support of my family.

I give thanks to my father, John, for his love and guidance over the years, and for helping me to believe and trust, even when you think you can't, that life does get better.

To my mother, Margaret, for her love and kind nature. She looked after everyone, not just me, and was a real friend to many.

My three brothers, Pat, Tom, and Pete. They are all very different, but each one of them has helped me and taken care of me.

Last but not least, to my little girl, Rosie, for bringing lots of love and happiness into my life, especially after my mother died when I was sixteen. Ann xx